caillou®

Watches Rosie

Adaptation from the animated series: Marion Johnson
Illustrations: CINAR Animation, adapted by Éric Sévigny

chouette

Caillou and Rosie are playing with Rosie's new toy.
They are having lots of fun — lots of noisy fun!
Every time Rosie pushes a key, the toy makes an
animal sound.

MOO! QUACK! ARF!

MEOW!

Mommy calls to them, "Children, you're making too much noise."

Caillou and Rosie stop what they are doing.

"Caillou, I need to lie down," says Mommy. "Can you be a good big brother and watch Rosie so she doesn't get into mischief?"

"Yes, Mommy," Caillou replies.

Mommy brings a couple of markers and two big pieces of paper.

"You and Rosie can draw pictures of the animals instead of listening to the sounds they make," she tells Caillou.

"I need you to play quietly so I can rest."

"Okay," says Caillou.

Caillou wants to help Mommy. He wants to be a good big brother. Caillou hands Rosie a marker and says, "We're going to draw now."
Caillou starts drawing a giraffe. He works so hard on his picture that he doesn't notice that Rosie is not drawing beside him.

Caillou looks around to see where Rosie went.
Oh, no! Rosie is drawing on the wall!
"Rosie! No!" shouts Caillou.

Caillou grabs the marker away from Rosie.
"No! No! Mine!" cries Rosie, and tries to get it back.
Caillou holds on to the marker. Rosie starts to cry.
"Be quiet!" Caillou tells her. "Do you want Mommy
to get mad?"

Mommy hears all the noise.
"Caillou," Mommy says, picking up Rosie, "I asked you to be a good big brother and watch Rosie, not fight with her. Rosie needs her nap. I'll be right back."

Caillou is surprised. Why is Mommy angry with him?
He did his best to be quiet and to keep Rosie from doing anything wrong.
He doesn't want to be Rosie's big brother any more!
When Mommy comes back, Caillou is crying.

Caillou and Mommy go to the kitchen and fill a bucket
with soap and water.
Mommy says, "It isn't easy being a big brother, is it?"
Caillou shakes his head. "Can I help?" he asks.
Mommy nods. "That would be great, Caillou."

Caillou cleans the wall with a wet cloth.
He rubs hard until all the marks are gone.
"Good work, Caillou! Thank you," says Mommy.

Rosie has finished her nap, and she wants Caillou
to play with her.
Caillou smiles and says, "Okay, Rosie."
Mommy gives Caillou a hug.
"Caillou, you are becoming such a big boy," she says.
"And you are such a good big brother to Rosie."

Text adapted by Marion Johnson based on the scenario of the CAILLOU animated film series produced by Cookie Jar Entertainment Inc. (© 1997 CINAR Productions (2004) Inc., a subsidiary of Cookie Jar Entertainment Inc.).
All rights reserved.
Original script written by Christel Kleitch.
Illustrations taken from the animated television series and adapted by Eric Sévigny.
Art Director: Monique Dupras

Bibliothèque et Archives nationales du Québec and Library and Archives Canada cataloguing in publication data

Johnson, Marion, 1949-
Caillou : watches Rosie
(Playtime)
Co-published by: Cookie Jar Entertainment Inc.
For children aged 3 and up.

ISBN 978-2-89450-635-6

1. Brothers and sisters - Juvenile literature. 2. Babysitting - Juvenile literature. I. Cookie Jar Entertainment Inc. II. Title. III. Series : Playtime (Montréal, Québec).

BF723.S43J63 2007   j306.875'3   C2007-940497-9

Legal deposit: 2007   b16268507

We acknowledge the financial support of the Government of Canada (Book Publishing Industry Development Program (BPIDP)) and the Government of Quebec (Tax credit for book publishing (SODEC)) for our publishing activities.